Dr. Wayne W. Dyer

with Kristina Tracy

Unstoppable Me!

10 Ways to Soar Through Life

Illustrated by **Stacy Heller Budnick**

HAY HOUSE, INC.
Carlsbad, California
London • Sydney • Johannesburg
Vancouver • Hong Kong • New Delhi

Published and distributed in the United States by: Hay House, Inc.: www.hayhouse.com • *Published and distributed in Australia by:* Hay House Australia Pty. Ltd.: www.hayhouse.com.au • *Published and distributed in the United Kingdom by:* Hay House UK, Ltd.: www.hayhouse. co.uk • *Published and distributed in the Republic of South Africa by:* Hay House SA (Pty), Ltd.: orders@psdprom.co.za • *Distributed in Canada by:* Raincoast: www.raincoast.com • *Published in India by:* Hay House Publications (India) Pvt. Ltd.: www.hayhouseindia.co.in • *Distributed in India by:* Media Star: booksdivision@mediastar.co.in

Design and Editorial Assistance: Jenny Richards • *Illustrations:* © Stacy Heller Budnick

Library of Congress Control Number: 2006923655

ISBN 13: 978-1-4019-1186-7
ISBN 10: 1-4019-1186-2

09 08 07 06   4 3 2 1
1st printing, October 2006

Printed in China

A Note from Wayne . . .

The work you're holding is based on my book for adults, *What Do You Really Want for Your Children?* in which I teach parents how they can lead their children, by example, to a happy and fulfilling life.

Each idea in *Unstoppable Me!* uses a rhyme to explain the concept and then has an example to illustrate how a child might use the lesson in his or her everyday life.

May you and your child enjoy reading and discussing these lessons together. There may be something to learn . . . for both of you!

What's Inside . . .

10 WAYS TO SOAR
THROUGH LIFE

1. You're Great—No Matter What!

2. Persistence Pays Off!

3. Welcome the Unknown

4. You Have a Choice

5. Farewell to Worry

6. Peace Begins with You

7. Enjoy the Here-and-Now

8. Healthy Me!

9. Creativity Is the Key!

10. What Can You Give?

Questions

#1
You're Great—
No Matter What!

You are worthwhile
simply because you're alive.
Never forget this
and you're sure to thrive.

Learn from your mistakes and
you'll get stronger as you grow.
Believe you'll succeed,
and then make it so.

If you value yourself
and all that you are—
you'll be unstoppable—
the next superstar!

I have a part in the big school play.
Unfortunately, I forgot all my lines today.
Some kids laughed, and I wanted to hide,
but I still believe I'm a star inside.
So tonight when I'm standing in that brilliant spotlignt,
no matter what happens, I'll be all right.

#2
Persistence Pays Off!

When there's something in your life
that you want to do,
once you begin,
you must follow through.

It's not about talent
or if you are smart;
it's about never quitting
something you start.

Don't tell yourself, "I can't,"
or dwell on mistakes;
patience and determination
are really all that it takes.

Every day after school I practice my guitar.
I know I can be just as good as any rock star.
I don't ever give up when my chords sound wrong.
I play them over and over till I nail that song!
My friends all say, "Can't you play something new?"
But to get where I want, I know what I have to do.

#3
Welcome the Unknown

Change is a good thing;
it happens every day—
if you learn this when you're young,
it will help you on your way.

Each day is different
from the day before,
and it sometimes feels scary
when opening a new door.

But if you don't fear change,
and embrace it instead,
life will be an adventure and
you'll look forward to what's ahead.

I've always spent the summer with my best friend, Shay,
but this year Mom sent me to sleepover camp—
which seemed so far away.
I cried and I yelled, "I won't know anyone!"
But Dad said, "Try it, I know you'll have such fun."
And guess what? He was right—I had nothing to fear.
I had such a blast that I'm going longer next year.

#4
You Have a Choice

Rely on yourself,
and be true to who you are.
What's unique about you
is what will take you far.

Don't look to others
to say you're okay.
You know it—so believe it!—
show your own self the way.

Don't blame others
for the things you say or do.
Every choice that you make
is all up to you.

Sometimes I think too much about what others do and say.
I feel so small around them—they must know the right way.
But then I stop and listen to that little inside voice,
the one that whispers in my heart, "You always have a choice."
So I pause and I think, *What's the best way for me?*
Only I know who and what I want to be.

TEACHER'S WAY

FRIEND'S WAY

BIG SISTER'S WAY

PARENT'S WAY

COACH'S WAY

MY WAY

#5
Farewell to Worry

If you want to be unstoppable,
there's something you must know:
Worrying can bring you down
and cause helpless feelings to grow.

Just try to remember,
when stressful thoughts attack,
that positive actions on your part
are the best way to fight back.

So talk to someone if you're feeling blue;
tell them about your thoughts.
Because sharing your burdens can help
you through many of life's rough spots.

Last night I was so worried about today's spelling test.
I could barely concentrate on studying, and I didn't get much rest.
So this morning when I woke up, I told my mom how I felt.
She gave me a hug, we practiced my words,
and my worries started to melt.
I'll do the best I possibly can, and that's enough for me.
It feels so good to take control—I feel confident and free.

#6
Peace Begins with You

If you want peace inside your heart,
don't let anger in.
It's just a feeling, after all;
it doesn't have to win.

When you're mad and let it change
the things you say and do,
not only do you hurt yourself,
but those around you, too.

So take your anger, let it go,
and learn to rise above—
then you can create a better world,
one filled with peace and love.

I was just watching some ants at work,
when out came my brother Tim.
He stepped on their hills, and I was so mad
I really wanted to hit him.
But instead, I hopped up on my swing
and let my anger fly away,
and thought of how my brother and I
could find a nice way to play.
I felt proud because I chose
the peaceful way to be.
When I have peace inside my heart,
life seems much better to me.

#7
Enjoy the Here-and-Now

Your past is now behind you,
and it has taught you many things.
You also have your future,
and you wonder what it will bring.

All these things to think about
can cause your head to spin,
so remember this key to happiness—
enjoy the moment that you're in!

Take pleasure in the here-and-now;
don't always be on the run.
The road you take to reach your goal
should be part of the fun!

Last week when I got a new kite, I took it out to fly,
but it was harder than it looked,
and I got mad when it didn't go high.
That's when my dad said, "Take a breath and slow it down a hair;
it's not just the goal that brings you joy—
it's the path you take to get there."
And when I stopped to look around, I saw that he was right.
I saw my family having fun, and the beautiful colors of my kite.

#8
Healthy Me!

Your body is amazing!
Pay attention and you'll find . . .
your body responds to what you think—
what you put inside your mind.

So tell yourself often,
"I'm healthy, and I'm strong!"
And if you happen to get sick,
know that you won't be for long.

Good thoughts and good humor
are truly the best start
for a super-healthy
mind, body, spirit, and heart.

I just love to play outside getting
exercise and fresh air.
My dog and I stay out until dark
when my Grandma calls, "Come in, Claire."
At dinner we sit down to my dad's spaghetti,
which I know is good for me.
While at the table, we talk and laugh
and enjoy our family.
When I go to bed, my body feels great
from everything I've done.
Taking care of my body and staying
healthy is actually lots of fun!

#9
Creativity Is the Key!

When it comes to your greatness,
creativity is the key,
because with it there's no limit
to what you can be.

Being creative can mean
so many things—
it's finding your own way to meet
the challenges life brings.

So if you have ideas for your
own way to shine,
just stay true to yourself
and you will do just fine.

I love to be different and wacky and wild.
Dad says I'm his creative child.
Like when I make a cake, it's unique and fun.
I don't always do things
the way they "should" be done.
It doesn't matter to me
if people think I am strange—
I am unstoppable—
and I don't need to change!

#10
What Can You Give?

What is a life full of meaning and purpose,
one that's truly limit free?
It's when you learn to look outside yourself
and not always think, *What about me?*

It means seeing goodness and
beauty everywhere you turn,
and taking every experience in life
as a chance for you to learn.

It's being at peace every day,
with a respect for all things that live
and not wondering what you can get,
but wondering what you can give.

"Dane," asked my grandpa, "what brings you joy?"
I answered, "Candy, of course, or a brand-new toy!"
He smiled at me and said, "I'm sure that is true,
but there is much more that can bring joy to you. . . .
Love and friendship and learning to give
will make your life fulfilling
and a pleasure to live."

Questions

The following pages have questions that relate to the ideas you have just read. Think about and answer these questions on your own, or with your parent or teacher, to learn how you can be unstoppable in your life!

Everyone has days where they make a mistake or do something embarrassing. Usually these things will turn out just fine and may even teach you a valuable lesson! Can you think of something you did that made you feel sad or embarrassed, but you kept a positive outlook and everything turned out better than you thought?

To be good at something requires persistence. That means sticking with it, no matter what! What is something you would like to be great at? How can persistence help you reach your goal?

Change will always be a part of life. The more you understand this, the easier your life will be. What are some things that have changed in your life lately, and what good things have come from these changes?

You can't always do things the way others want you to. Every person on Earth is unique and can only be truly happy if they follow their own inner wisdom. That wisdom, or little voice inside, can help you make decisions that are right for you. Do you ever feel something inside guiding you in your choices?

Worrying is something we all do from time to time, but it doesn't really help anything. What does help is talking to someone or coming up with a plan! What is something you worry about? Have you talked to anyone about your thoughts? What other actions can you take to tackle your fears?

Anger can be a very powerful emotion. What you choose to do with this feeling affects you and the people around you. When you start to notice your anger building up, what can you do to help it go away and feel peaceful inside?

Questions

It's exciting to look forward to the future. You have so much ahead of you! But to get the most out of life, you must learn to notice what's going on around you. Look around you right now. What are three things you can appreciate about this very moment?

Playing outside and eating good food are great ways to keep your body healthy. But did you know that laughing, enjoying life, and keeping your thoughts positive are also good for your body? What do you do to keep your body healthy? What do you do to keep your mind healthy?

When you do kind and generous things for others, it not only helps them, but will make you feel happier, too. Can you think of a time when you did something loving or kind for another person, or even an animal? How did it make you feel inside?

Being creative is when you think beyond the usual way of doing things. It's when you reach inside your mind for your own unique ideas and answers. Can you think of a time when you came up with your own creative way to do something? Did it make you feel special? Proud? What else?

We hope you enjoyed this Hay House book.
If you'd like to receive a free catalog featuring additional Hay House books and products,
or if you'd like information about the Hay Foundation, please contact:

Hay House, Inc.
P.O. Box 5100
Carlsbad, CA 92018-5100

(760) 431-7695 or (800) 654-5126
(760) 431-6948 (fax) or (800) 650-5115 (fax)
www.hayhouse.com® • www.hayfoundation.org

Published and distributed in Australia by: Hay House Australia Pty. Ltd., 18/36 Ralph St.,
Alexandria NSW 2015 • Phone: 612-9669-4299 • Fax: 612-9669-4144 • www.hayhouse.com.au

Published and distributed in the United Kingdom by: Hay House UK, Ltd., 292B Kensal Rd.,
London W10 5BE • Phone: 44-20-8962-1230 • Fax: 44-20-8962-1239 • www.hayhouse.co.uk

Published and distributed in the Republic of South Africa by: Hay House SA (Pty), Ltd., P.O. Box 990,
Witkoppen 2068 • Phone/Fax: 27-11-706-6612 • orders@psdprom.co.za

Published in India by: Hay House Publications (India) Pvt. Ltd. • www.hayhouseindia.co.in

Distributed in India by: Media Star, 7 Vaswani Mansion, 120 Dinshaw Vachha Rd., Churchgate,
Mumbai 400020 • Phone: 91 (22) 22815538-39-40 • Fax: 91 (22) 22839619 • booksdivision@mediastar.co.in

Distributed in Canada by: Raincoast, 9050 Shaughnessy St., Vancouver, B.C. V6P 6E5 •
Phone: (604) 323-7100 • Fax: (604) 323-2600 • www.raincoast.com

Tune in to **HayHouseRadio.com**® for the best in
inspirational talk radio featuring top Hay House authors!

And, sign up via the Hay House USA Website to receive
the Hay House online newsletter and stay informed
about what's going on with your favorite authors.
You'll receive bimonthly announcements about: Dis-
counts and Offers, Special Events, Product Highlights,
Free Excerpts, Giveaways, and more!
www.hayhouse.com®